mike Payne
Ole Police Buddy and Friend

# ELMER the Dancing Turtle

## Lonie B. Adcock

*Lonie B Adcock*

*Lonie B. Adcock*

# Elmer the Dancing Turtle

## ©2013 by Lonie B. Adcock

## A Taylors Ridge Book

TRAudiobookRecording.com

Printed and also published by

Lulu.com

### First Edition

### ISBN 978-1-300-42382-9

*Lonie B. Adcock*

# Introduction

After seeing and reading some of the books that are out there for young children, I decided to try my hand at a book that a small child could look at and read that would be suitable. There are, in my opinion, so many books that teach small children words that, to me, are unfit for small ears. In the early stages of life, when they should be taught, they are often given words and things that should not be put in front of them. This book is totally of my opinions and is subject to be disagreed upon by some. I still believe in God, Family, Country, and the American way of life.

All characters in this story are figments of my imagination. There is no intent to show them as being real. A story like this could not be real. Can you imagine a turtle that danced? Look around you, and there is a chance that you can find someone who looks and acts like Elmer's friends.

**Lonie B. Adcock**

*Lonie B. Adcock*

# Acknowledgments

Dr. Russ Delaino who encouraged me to continue writing.

To E. Wayne, an old Policeman Buddy who had bigger ears than me.

To the Kellys of Main Street Bookstore in Cedartown, Georgia. Kevin made Elmer come alive with his cartoon drawing.

I wish to thank Dale Jackson Early Jr. for giving me Bucky the Bully Beaver.

# Family and Friends of Elmer Turtle

Roscoe Turtle          Lulu Turtle (Parents)

Hiram Turtle          Myrtle Turtle (Siblings)

Stinky and Inky Skunk

Fluffy and Muffin Rabbit

Hoot and Toot Owl

Professor Hootie Owl

Freddy and Edie Frog

Cal and Al Muskrat

Bucky Beaver

Munch and Crunch Woodchuck

Hiss the King Snake

Doctor Foggers Frog

Ham Hamster

Nick and Charlie Mouse

# Family and Friends (cont.)

Joe and Josie Turtle

Ollie and Mollie Oppossum

Billie and Willie Goat

John, Smarty, and Foxie Fox

Polly Parrot

King Harrell

Queen Vanna

Princess Sunshine

Doctor Wood Woodie

Commander Odum

Bennie and Minnie Turtle

***The next dancing turtle, Hiram's Little Elmer***

# Table of Contents

*Lonie B. Adcock*

# Elmer

# the Dancing Turtle

## Lonie B. Adcock

Roscoe and Lulu Turtle sat perfectly still, staring at the eggs lying in the basket. They held hands as they sat and watched, not saying a word. Then, as if on signal, one of the eggs moved. Roscoe squeezed Lulu's hand and started to say something, but the egg stopped moving, and he sat quiet again. Silence. Not a sound anywhere. And then one of the eggs rolled over and stood up on its end. The shell began to crack, and Roscoe looked at Lulu with excitement showing on his face. Then the shell fell off, revealing a small figure. Lulu grabbed it up and began to clean the fragment of shell from it. Then another egg stood up on its end, and the shell began to crack, leaving another small figure. Roscoe grabbed the small figure and started to clean up all the pieces of shell from it.

Roscoe and Lulu held the small figures in their hands, admiring them. Then a noise from the basket drew their attention back to the basket and the third egg. The egg had begun to roll over and, to their surprise, had begun to jump up and down. This was more than Roscoe could stand. He reached down and picked up the egg. Holding it close to his ear, he began to listen. Shaking his head, he put the egg back into the basket.

"Mama," he said, looking at Lulu.

"Yes?" she said with a surprised look on her face.

Roscoe pointed to the egg, shaking his head, saying, "What is the matter with the egg?"

Lulu smiled. "Give it time, Papa. It will be okay."

**Lulu and Roscoe Turtle**

The egg began to tremble and roll around in the basket. Mama Turtle began to clean all the eggshells out of the basket, and she laid the little ones on a small pillow. Roscoe and Lulu watched them as they came to life.

Papa said, "Look, Lulu," pointing to the little ones on the pillow. "What do you see, Mama?" he asked, turning and looking at the two on the pillow.

"There," Lulu said, pointing to them again, "See?" she said. "That one is a boy, and the other one is a girl."

"I see, Mama," Roscoe said, with pride in his voice. "I think I will call him *Hiram* after his great grandfather."

"Wait," Lulu said, "for I intend to call her Myrtle after my grandmother."

"That is good," Roscoe said. "Those are two good names." He reached over and took Lulu's hand while admiring the little ones.

Then the egg in the basket stood up on its end and began to bounce around. It bounced across the basket from one side to the other and then rolled to the middle and lay still. Roscoe drew in a deep breath. The egg began to crack, and a foot came though the shell. Then to their amazement, another foot came though the shell. Smiles appeared on Roscoe's and Lulu's faces. They knew the little one in the shell was okay.

The shell split open, and out came a little one, and he was dancing across the basket in front of them. His little feet were doing what everyone called *the waltz*. He stopped in front of Lulu and bowed, and then he moved over to Roscoe and bowed.

He stepped back several steps and bowed again, and then to their amazement, he said, "Mama! Papa!" And started to dance back across the basket.

That was all Lulu could take. She reached down and picked him up.

A big smile came on his face, and he said, "Mama!"

Lulu's heart did a double beat, and she put him against her, hugging him tightly.

Roscoe beamed with pride. It was there in a loving home with a loving family Elmer the Dancing Turtle was born.

# The Early Years

Roscoe and Lulu settled in to raising a family. Where most families were blessed with two, Roscoe and Lulu had received three. It didn't matter, for the love in their hearts would have covered three more. Lulu and Roscoe would dress them in their best and take them to the park. Elmer was liked by all the other children. While Hiram and Myrtle would be playing on the playground equipment, Elmer would have a group of the girls dancing with him. He was quite popular with the girls.

Elmer was different from all the rest of the children to the point that he had become a novelty in the community.

Roscoe was often asked by the other parents of children, "Does he dance everywhere he goes?"

In fact, he did, to the dismay of Roscoe and Lulu, but they had become accustomed to him around the house, dancing instead of walking.

It worried Roscoe so much that he consulted Professor Hootie Owl. Professor Hootie was without a doubt the wisest one in the community. He taught all the children in school, and it was known throughout the community if you had a problem, go see him.

After giving it much thought, they went to the office of Professor Hootie. He met them with a warm greeting.

"Come in, Mister and Mrs. Turtle," he said. After a few words between them, he asked "And now, what seems to be your problem?"

Roscoe looked at Lulu who was looking at him. Roscoe cleared his throat, for he knew that the burden of telling Professor Hootie the problem was his.

"It's this way," he said, clearing his throat again. "Our son, Elmer. He dances all the time. If he goes somewhere, he dances there. In the house he dances from room to room. Professor Hootie, we are afraid that there is something the matter with him."

A perplexed look came on Hootie's face. He took his hand and reached over and took a cloth from the table beside him. With the look still on his face, he wiped his forehead. He looked at them, shaking his head.

"You say he dances everywhere he goes?"

"Yes," Lulu answered. "He never stops. His feet are always moving."

"Always?" Professor Hootie asked.

"Always," Lulu said, shaking her head. "Papa and I watch him while he is asleep. His feet move."

"Hmm," Professor Hootie said. "Very strange. Have you had old Doctor Foggers check him?"

Old Doctor Foggers Frog was, as everyone knew, the best doctor for miles around.

"Yes," Lulu answered. "The Doctor said he appeared normal except for the dancing."

Professor Hootie got up, walked over to his desk in the corner of the room, picked up a pair of glasses, and put them on. This made him look old and very wise.

Then, to the surprise of Lulu and Roscoe, he began to pace back and forth.

He came to a sudden stop and said, "Lulu, Roscoe, I am going to tell you something that happened to me early in life. If I ever hear a word of this from anyone, I will deny it. Understand?"

Lulu and Roscoe looked at each other and then shook their heads to let the Professor know that they would not tell anyone else.

He turned and walked over to his chair and sat down.

"This happened to me when I was a little fellow about the age of your Elmer. I came into this world dancing as he did. I danced my way through childhood. When I started to school, my parents decided that the dancing had to go. I was sent to a private tutor so they could get the dancing out of me.

"My parents would say, 'Whoever heard of a dancing owl? Owls are wise.' They wanted me to become a professor and help out people. Much to my battered pride, I became a professor.

"Now *my* advice is help your son and give him all the encouragement you can. Let him become what he wants to. There is a chance that he will outgrow the dancing and become something else." He removed his glasses and again wiped his forehead.

Roscoe stood up, knowing that they had gotten all the advice they were going to get from Professor Hootie.

On the way back home they didn't speak a word between them. They were both deep in their own thoughts. Once at home they sat in chairs facing the window and watched the children play. Hiram and Myrtle were running normally, but Elmer, as usual, was dancing.

"Mama," Roscoe said, "do you think he will grow out of it?"

"Papa, we can only hope," she answered.

"Very well," Roscoe said. "We will be patient and do what we have to so he will grow up to be normal."

When Lulu and Roscoe had left Professor Hootie's office, he walked over to a closet and took out a box. He placed it on his desk and removed the top from it. He stood and looked at the contents with a faraway look in his eyes. Then he reached over and took out a pair of shoes. The shoes were red and had taps on them. They were dancing shoes. He picked them up and held them in his hands, staring at them with tears in his eyes. They were his dancing shoes that he had worn back when he was young. He put them down and picked up a red shirt from the box. He gently laid it beside the shoes. A pair of black pants came next, followed by a coat with tails. He placed them on the desk and reached into the box and took out a white scarf. There appeared to be tears in his eyes as he looked at the contents of the box. He got up and moved over to the closet.

Reaching up on a shelf, he took down a small top hat. Turning, he placed it on the desk. With a solemn look he sat and stared at the items on the desk. As he stared at the red shoes, his feet began to move. Then he stood up and began to dance. He had always wanted to dance and had never forgotten how. He often danced when he was alone.

Time passed, and Elmer showed no sign that he was going to quit dancing. Roscoe and Lulu encouraged him, and he sent off for a course in professional dancing. He had taps placed on his shoes, and you could hear him when he got near. He became quite a novelty  in the little village. They got used to seeing him and would gather around to watch. Then the day approached that Roscoe and Lulu were worried about.

*Lonie B. Adcock*

# School Days

Lulu took Hiram, Myrtle, and Elmer to school the first day. Hiram and Myrtle walked along beside Lulu while Elmer danced along in front of her. As they walked to the schoolhouse, the other parents were walking along with their youngsters. The mothers were talking while the kids ran along, playing. It was a sight to see. The sidewalk was full of all kinds of creatures headed for Professor Hootie's school.

Professor Hootie, decked out in his robe and hat, stood watching as they approached the school. He knew he was in for another trying year, but he enjoyed teaching the little ones. As the first little ones entered, he put on his glasses. He didn't really need glasses, but he wore them because it made him look distinguished. They began to file in, and he directed them to the seats that he wanted them to sit in.

With everyone seated, Professor Hootie cleared his throat. Clearing his throat was the way that the Professor had to get their attention.

"Welcome everyone," he said, as he looked them over. "So as there will be no misunderstanding between your parents and me, I will have my say now. Some of you have heard it before, but for those of you who haven't, I will say it again. You will pay attention while in my classroom. All questions will be answered by me at the end of the lesson."

He looked at the small ones sitting in the room and said, "We will start with this row, and you will come to the front of the room and introduce yourself." Pointing to the first two that were seated, he said, "You first."

They came forward and bowed to the professor.

"My name is Earl Squirrel."

Smiling, the other one said, "I am Earl's sister, Pearl."

They turned and walked back to their seat.

25

"Next," the professor said.

Two more got up and came forward, bowing to the professor.

"I am Cal Muskrat," one of them said. Smiling, he pointed to the other one.

"I am Al," he said. "Cal is my brother."

They went back to their seat.

**Bucky Beaver**

"Next," the professor said.

A slight shuffle of feet, and he got up. He came to the front, and unlike the others, he sneered at the professor.

With a fist, he said, "I am Bucky Beaver. I am the toughest creature in the village, and no one dares *not* do what I ask." With a sneer he turned and walked back to his seat.

The parents looked at him in disbelief, for they could not believe what they had heard.

The little creatures sat with a stunned look on their faces. You could see that what he had said had its effect on them.

"Next," the professor said. Two more got up and came to the front, bowing to the professor. Turning to the others in the room one of them said, "I am Munch Woodchuck.

The other one said, "I am Crunch Woodchuck, the brother of Munch. If the big bad Beaver wants to get munched and crunched, let him mess with the Woodchuck Brothers.

Smiling at the others in the room, they walked over to Bucky Beaver and with a smile on their faces bowed.

"Next," the professor said.

**Fluffy Rabbit**

**Muffin Rabbit**

Down the aisle they came with their little fluffy tails just bouncing. They hopped to the front and bowed to the professor.

He smiled, thinking what a group of beautiful little creatures he had to teach.

They turned to the others in the room.

"I am Fluffy Rabbit," one of them said.

"I am his sister, Muffin Rabbit, and we are glad to be here with all of you."

All the parents in the room smiled at them as they came back to their seats.

"Next," the professor said. He beamed as two little owls came down the aisle and to the front of the room. The reason he beamed was that they were his grand-creatures. They came to the professor and stopped, looking up at him. They then turned to the others in the room.

"I am Hoot," one of them said. "Professor Hootie is my grandfather." He is the best grandfather in the world!"

"I am Toot," the other one said, "Grandpa's little princess."

The professor beamed as they turned going back to their seats.

"Next," the professor said.

Everyone turned and looked down at the floor and to their amazement saw a small black Snake heading to the front of the room. He stopped and made a hissing sound. A shuffle of feet, and the professor held up his hand.

"It's okay," the professor said. "Hiss is a friendly King Snake. He will harm no one. He will be enrolled in our class this year. Go ahead," the professor said to Hiss.

"I am Hiss," he said. "I am what humans call a King Snake. We do not harm any animals or humans, but we will chase away those who wish to harm you."

They all watched as Hiss went back to his seat, still a little leery of a snake among their little ones. They trusted Professor Hootie, so they relaxed and waited for the others.

"Next," the professor said.

They watched as two small frogs came up the aisle. Once in front of the professor they bowed. They then turned to the room.

"I am Freddie the frog," he said with a croak.

"I am Edie the sister of Freddie. We are twins, but I am prettier than he is." She turned and smiled at Freddie and then started back to her seat.

This brought laughter from the parents in the room, and they looked at the mother. She smiled at them, letting them know that she was proud of Freddie and Edie.

"Next," the professor said as Freddie and Edie sat down.

## Walter the Duck

A slap of funny sounding feet hit the floor, and all the animals in the room turned to see who was next. It was Walter the Duck. What they had heard was Walter's toenails, for he was barefooted. Like all ducks, Walter waddled as he walked, and being barefooted his toenails scratched the floor.

He stopped in front of the professor and said, "Quack, quack!" and bowed. Then he turned to the others and said, "I am Walter the Duck. Mom calls me her little man while dad calls me lazy." He let out a loud "quack" and waddled back to his seat.

"Next," the professor said.

The sound of tiny feet could be heard as they came forward. The two little ones approached the professor, bowed, and then turned to the room.

"I am Bill Opossum."

"I am Sill, his sister, and no one had better make fun of my name." You could hear a pin drop as they returned to their seats.

"Next," the professor said.

The others in the room were getting tired and were wishing that this was over with.

As these two approached the front, the professor took a couple of steps backwards. They approached him and bowed.

Turning to the room one of them giggled. The one that giggled spoke. "I am known to all as Stinky the Skunk. It is not a good idea to make me mad."

The other one spoke. "I am Inky, Stinky's sister. Stinky was only kidding with you, for he is not harmful."

Stinky spoke, looking at Bucky Beaver. "If anyone is bothered by the village bully, let me know."

As they walked back to their seats, Stinky ran down the aisle to where Bucky sat. Stinky grabbed his tail in his hand and put it in  Bucky's face. Bucky let out a yell and, jumping to his feet, ran to the front of the room.

"Here, here!" the professor yelled. "We will have none of that."

**Inky and Stinky**

Stinky giggled and said, "Shucks! Didn't even have my tail wet, and he runs and screams."

The parents in the room laughed while the children beat on the desks and hoorayed. Bucky dropped his head and walked back to his desk.

As he sat down, he was heard to say, "I will get even with all of you, for I am the toughest one in all of the village."

A loud laugh went up among the little creatures in the room. Bucky sat still and never said another word. Professor Hootie looked puzzled and at loss for words. He removed his glasses and began cleaning them with a cloth he took from his pocket. The room grew quiet. He cleared his throat and put his glasses on.

He spoke, saying, "Next."

Then from the back of the room came Hiram and Myrtle Turtle. A clicking of taps, and everyone knew Elmer was up and dancing.

Hiram came first, bowing to the professor, saying, "I am Hiram Turtle. Here with me is my sister, Myrtle. This is my brother, Elmer."

Elmer danced across to the professor and bowed. The Turtles then went back to their seats, Elmer dancing in front of them.

Professor Hootie spoke. "You may all be dismissed for the rest of the day. I will see you all here in the morning. Classes will begin at 8 o'clock sharp. If by chance any one is late, your parents will be notified. Dismissed!"

With a loud cheer the children began to run outside, followed by their parents. A tapping noise caused Professor Hootie to turn and look at the back of the room. Elmer was just getting up, and his feet were moving at a speed that caused Professor Hootie to stare in admiration.

He did a bow as he danced by the professor. The professor watched as he danced out and joined his parents. With a sad look on his face, he closed the door and walked over and sat down at his desk.

*Yes sir,* he thought. Come morning he had his job cut out for him. He leaned back in his chair and closed his eyes. He could see the dancing feet of Elmer in his mind.

Professor Hootie was up early the next morning. He had his breakfast and immediately went down to the school and opened the doors so the kids could get in when they came.

The wait wasn't long before they began to file in. When he thought that everyone was in, he went over and closed the door. He turned back to the room when he heard a tapping outside. He turned, opening the door. Elmer came dancing through.

He smiled as Elmer came dancing by him.

"Glad you could make it."

"Sorry I am late, sir."

"That is fine, not late enough for it to hurt anything. Be on time from now on."

"Won't happen again, sir," he said as he sat down.

The Professor turned his attention back to the room. He wiped his glasses and then put them on. He cleared his throat and walked over to what looked like a rolled up window shade. He reached and started to pull it down.

**Jesus**

They sat still. Not a sound could be heard. Slowly the shade came down. Not a sound was made as the face of a human appeared on the shade .The face had a beard and long hair. Light seem to come from the face as he looked upward. They watched as the professor turned toward them. He reached down and picked up his pointer. Again he cleared his throat. They found out later he cleared his throat to get their attention.

"Does anyone recognize whose picture this is?"

"No?" he said, turning toward them.

"I do," a small voice said coming from the back of the room.

"Who was that," he asked, "that said they knew?"

"Me, sir."

Everyone turned to see who had said they knew who the face was on the picture. Everyone knew as soon as they heard the toe taps on the shoes hit the floor that it was Elmer.

"How would you know whose picture this is?" the Professor asked.

"It is a picture of Christ, the son of God."

"You are right, but who is God?"

**Professor Hootie**

"God is the creator of the universe. He created the universe and all of the creatures that live in it. The same picture hangs on the wall of the building that has the steeple on top of it."

"What were you doing in that building?"

"Mama and Papa carry us down there every Sunday."

"Good for Mama and Papa Turtle," the professor said.

The rest of the day was taken up on getting acquainted with each other and future studies. A recess was given after a period of time, and they went outside to play. As usual, Elmer had the center of attention with his dancing feet.

As they gathered around Elmer, Bucky stood on the side with a sneer on his face.

"I will show that smart turtle who is the toughest," he said as he walked toward where Elmer was.

He began to shove and push everyone out of the way as he walked toward Elmer. They parted as he approached Elmer. Elmer kept dancing, ignoring him. Everyone could tell that Bucky wasn't used to being ignored.

Bucky let out a loud snarl and jumped at Elmer. With a smile on his face Elmer sidestepped him, and Bucky hit the ground. A loud roar of laughter went up from the crowd. Bucky just barely hit the ground and was back on his feet.

"No one does that to me!" he yelled at the top of his voice.

Then Elmer did something that surprised all that were watching. He began to do back flips. He did several, landing on his feet, and then began to dance around Bucky. Bucky stood with a stunned look on his face, and then he let out another yell. The crowd began to move back and it was just Elmer left facing him. He began to close in on Elmer. Elmer backed in against a wall and couldn't move any farther. A moan went up among the crowd as they began to move toward Bucky.

Then above the noise of the crowd a voice said, "Hold it, everyone."

There to the surprise of everyone came Inky and Stinky Skunk with their tails in their hands. They advanced on Bucky. He began to move away from Elmer. Inky and Stinky kept coming. Bucky started to move back from Elmer, but they kept closing in on him.

"Go away, you guys!" he yelled.

They rushed him, fanning him with their tails. With a scream that could have been heard a mile, he turned and fled off of the school ground and down the street. A roar of laughter followed him as he left. The ringing of the school bell called them back inside.

The years slowly passed without any aggression from anyone. All students passed all their classes with honors, and soon it would be graduation time.

Professor Hootie looked on his class with admiration. It wouldn't be too long before they would be out of school. It was time to start the class's preparing for the prom. They always had a play with the students showing off their special talents. He had them going through their parts now to make sure that when prom night got here they would be ready. He went and looked into the auditorium. Elmer was on stage practicing a routine, and the professor watched with interest. A sad look was on his face. Elmer finished, and Professor Hootie called to him.

"Elmer?"

"Yes, sir."

Elmer, would you come into my office?"

"Yes, sir," Elmer said, following Professor Hootie into his office.

"Have a seat, son. I want to show you something that is dear to my heart."

Elmer watched as Professor Hootie went over to the closet and opened it. He reached in taking out a cane and a top hat. He placed them on his desk. He then went back to the closet taking out clothes that were wrapped in shiny fabric. Going back to the closet he reached in and brought out a red pair of shoes with taps on the toes.

Elmer's heart almost stopped beating, for this was the prettiest pair of shoes he had ever seen. He watched as the professor placed the clothes and put the shoes on the desk.

"Come," he motioned to Elmer.

Elmer got up and slowly approached the desk.

"What do you think of them?" the professor asked.

"They are beautiful!"

"Would you like to have them?"

"Oh, yes, sir, more than anything in this world!"

"Try them on. If they fit, you can have them," the professor said, leaving the room.

Elmer tried the pants first. A perfect fit. Next came the shirt and jacket. Another perfect fit as if they were made for him. He picked up the shoes, Going over to a chair he sat down. Taking off his shoes he tried on the red shoes. He stood up in them. They felt like he had always worn them. He danced over to the desk, picking up the scarf. He put it around his neck. He looked in a mirror that was on the wall, and a big smile lit up his face. Then to his surprise his feet began to dance. He picked up the hat and stick and danced. He was so taken up by his dancing that he hadn't noticed that the professor was standing in the door, watching him. When he saw the professor watching him, he stopped.

"No, no my boy," the professor said. "Go ahead."

The professor sat down, and Elmer started back to dancing. He danced like he had never danced in his life. A smile was on the face of the professor as he watched.

When Elmer had finished, he stopped in front of the professor and bowed with a smile on his face.

"Bravo, my boy. Do that tonight, and you are sure to be the winner of the contest."

"Do you think so, sir?"

"No doubt in my mind as to who will be the winner."

"The clothes and shoes, sir, I will take them off and give them back to you."

"The outfit is yours. Take it, and every time you dance, remember me."

"Yes, sir, I sure will, and each time I dance, it will be for you."

"Take the outfit off, and let no one see it until you come out on stage tonight. That will give everyone the surprise of their life."

With a big smile on his face he began to change back into his clothes and to fold and put up the dancing outfit that the professor had given him.

"Thank you, sir," he said, as he danced through the door and back to the auditorium.

"You are welcome, and show them what you can do tonight," the professor said, as Elmer danced through the door.

**Smarty Fox**

# The Promoter

Smarty Fox was tired, he was hungry, and to make things worse, his car was hot and boiling over. He could see a village just ahead of him. Maybe he could find a garage there and find someone who could fix his car. Then he saw the sign: "Billie and Willie Auto Repair Shop. His car quit just as he turned in the driveway. He let it coast on in to the shop. A car sat in the aisle with the hood up, and he could see two figures working under the hood. He got out and walked over to the car. They hadn't seen him when he came in. They were having a conversation. He stopped and listened.

"Now, Willie, you are wrong. It is the carburetor."

*Lonie B. Adcock*

# Willie & Billie Goat

## The Best Mechanics in the Whole World

"Billy you think you know everything, anyone can see that it the distributor cap."

Smarty cleared his throat, making a loud noise. The two on the car jumped hitting their heads on the hood.

A loud yell, and they hit the ground holding their heads. They stop hollering, still rubbing their heads.

"Who are you?" asked the one who was holding a wrench.

"Gentlemen, I am Smarty the Fox. I am a promoter."

"You are who? And you do what?" the one holding the wrench asked again.

"I am Smarty the Fox. I make famous stars out of ordinary creatures."

"I am Willie, and this is my brother, Billy. We are the Goat Boys, the smartest mechanics in the whole wide world."

He put the wrench down and turned to look at Smarty's car. He walked over to it and raised the hood. Billie went over and looked at the motor. "Easy to see what is the trouble."

"What do you think is the trouble?" Willie asked.
"Easy to see it is the water pump."

"Come here, Willie," He motioned to his brother.

Moving over to where he could see the motor, he again said, "Water pump."

"Not so." Willie said.

"Is so," Billy said.

The two were going at it. Smarty walked between the two. He looked at first one and then the other.

"Stop it!" he yelled. "Just tell me if you can fix my car."

"Why, there is no use to get all excited. Billy and I can fix anything. We are the best mechanics in the whole world."

"Stop talking and get to fixing then," Smarty said, walking out the door.

Willie shook his head. "Come on, Billy. Let's get this water pump off."

"Not the water pump," Billy said.

Smarty Fox walked up the street, taking in the small village. He was getting a little hungry and started looking for a place to eat. There on the corner he saw a sign that said, "Eats--The Best in the Village." On the window in bold letters a sign said, "Big Bear Eatery." He pushed open the door and walked in. He stopped just inside, letting his eyes adjust to the dark room. There were several couples sitting at tables, eating. He walked over to a table and sat down.

A waitress came over and put a menu on the table. She said, "My name is Polly Parrot. I will be your waitress."

She left, returning with a glass of water. He ordered and then began to look around. He saw nothing of interest, so he reached over to the table next to him and picked up a paper. He opened it up and began to read. Nothing of interest. He then laid the paper down in a chair as his food arrived. He ate slowly, wondering how long he would have to stay in this hick village. Then out of the corner of his eye he saw something in the paper that looked interesting. He picked up the paper and began to read.

"Tonight is the night that the graduates of Village High will graduate. They have all been waiting for this. After the graduating ceremony, a show of talent will begin. The students will show off their talents in different categories. The show is free, so come one come all."

He walked outside and at the end of the block saw the auditorium. He would get there in time to see the whole group of talent. Who knows? He might find someone in the crowd who could make it big. After all, he was a talent scout, and that was what had brought him to this neck of the woods.

The auditorium was dark as he entered. He slowly worked his way as close to the front as possible. He slid into a seat and leaned back, relaxed. A small girl rabbit was singing, and he immediately decided she would not make it big in the outside world. He sat through a group of singers, jugglers, acrobats, and who only knows what else. He was just about to give it up and go check on his car when his attention was caught by a black robed figure entering the stage.

The auditorium grew quiet as Professor Hootie stepped out on the stage.

"Now this act is one fellow that we all are familiar with. He has danced his way into all of our hearts here in the village." He was an A student, but he couldn't keep his feet still, but we grew used to that. Here he is-- Elmer the dancing turtle."

Smarty sat up. A dancing turtle? He had to see this. The lights went down, and a spot was thrown onto the stage. It moved to one side as the music started. Then from behind the curtain a hat came into view. Then to the amazement of all, a walking stick came out beside the hat. Next a pair of red shoes came into view. Then to the delight of all, Elmer came from behind the curtain. He danced his heart out for the creatures. They cheered him on. When it was over and he danced back behind the curtain, the crowd went wild.

The audience stood up and yelled, "More, more! We want Elmer! We want Elmer!"

Elmer came out on the stage and bowed. The music started, and Elmer began to dance. The audience grew quiet not making a noise of any kind. The taps on his shoes could be heard over the music.

Smarty Fox sat watching stunned. He had traveled everywhere hunting talent. He had never seen any that could come close to the dancing turtle. He watched, looking around, and taking in the faces in the audience. Like them, he was also stunned.

The music stopped, and again the audience went wild, yelling, "Elmer! Elmer!"

Professor Hootie came out on the stage and the crowd grew quiet.

"This, ladies and gentlemen, is the end of our presentation of talent." I hope you have enjoyed the performance and remember them in the future."

He made a motion with his hand, and the curtain began to close. Everyone got up and began to file out of the auditorium. Smarty Fox sat still until everyone was out of the auditorium. Once the aisle was cleared, he got up and headed to the back of the stage. A door on the side of the stage led up behind the curtain. He opened the door and stepped through. Elmer and his family, along with Professor Hootie, were standing in the center of the stage. They were congratulating Elmer on his performance.

They turned toward Smarty as he came through the door. Professor Hootie turned to him and asked, "Is there something that we can do for you sir?"

"Yes," Smarty said, "I wish to speak to the young fellow who did the dancing on the stage."

"That was me," Elmer said.

Smarty began to talk. "Young man, that was some of the best dancing that I have ever seen." My name is Smarty Fox. I am a promoter." He handed a card to Roscoe.

Roscoe took the card, looked at it, and passed it over to Lulu. Lulu looked at it and handed it to Professor Hootie. He looked at it and then handed it to Elmer, who was watching with a surprised look on his face.

"What does this mean?" Elmer asked.

"It means that I can make you rich and famous," Smarty answered.

"Rich and what?" Elmer asked.

"Famous," Smarty said with a big smile on his face. "Rich and famous with more money than your family could every spend."

Elmer didn't say anything. He looked at his father and remembered how hard Roscoe worked to make a living for them. Roscoe and Lulu deserved the good life, and if he could give it to them, he would do so.

Professor Hootie spoke up saying, "Let's go in to my office where we can sit down and discuss this."

They  followed him in to his office. They all took a chair and were seated. The only empty chair was in the middle of them. Elmer walked over and sat down.

"Now, you say you make this young man famous and he can make a fortune?" Hootie asked. "Tell us how you intend to do this and what young Elmer would have to do."

"He would have to dance on stage in a big theater."

"On stage in a big theater in front of an audience?" Hootie, asked.

"He would have to leave Smallville and home?" Lulu wanted to know.

"He would have to leave Smallville and home. He would have a good place to live with all the food he wanted."

"What about his dancing?" Roscoe asked.

Smarty said, "That is where his fame and fortune comes  in. He would be paid to do what he is enjoying, and that is *dancing.*"

They looked at Elmer, for they could see that he was taking it all in.

He hadn't said a word, but now he spoke. "I would be paid to dance on  stage in front of an audience?" He grew quiet. They knew what he was thinking about.

Smarty watched Elmer. He knew what was in his mind. Leaving home and your loved ones was always hard to do for a young fellow just starting out. He remained quiet, for he knew the decision to go to the big village was his decision. If he didn't go on his own, he would never make it away from home.

Elmer looked at Smarty and asked him, "If I go with you, when will I get paid so that my family will have some money?"

"With your parents' approval and the contract signed, you will receive your first payment. As you perform, your money will get bigger. If at the end of your contract you decide not to keep on dancing, you can quit."

"That is the question. How long of a contract do you require?" the professor asked.

Smarty reached into an inside pocket of his coat and pulled out a paper. He handed it to Professor Hootie.

"This, sir, is a standard contract for two years."

He took the paper and unfolded it. He reached up and pulled his glasses down over his eyes. No one said anything. They sat and watched the professor. He made no attempt to get in a hurry. He read it slowly, studying it as he went along. He got up and moved around to his desk. He placed the paper into a typewriter and began to type. He paused, studying what he had written. He got up and came back to Smarty.

"Here, sir, are the terms of the contract if Elmer agrees to come back home."

Smarty read what the professor had written at the bottom of the page.

"Agree, sir," he said.

"Good," the professor said. "Now run along we have a lot of discussion to do. Where, sir, are you staying? I would suggest you get a room at the Happy Nook Rest Inn. Meet us back here in the morning, and we will give you your answer as to whether Elmer will go with you."

Smarty got to his feet. "Very good," he said. "I will see you here in the morning."

He stepped out onto the sidewalk and looked around. He saw his car sitting outside of the Goat boys' garage. He started down the sidewalk toward the garage. He felt good, for he knew that if he got Elmer to the big village he had it made. There was no doubt in his mind that Elmer would become a hit in the big villages.

The Goat brothers watched as he approached. Willie looked at Billy and whispered, "He looks like a con artist to me."

"Hush," Billy said. "He might hear you. I have told you to never judge a creature by his appearance."

"Anyway, he seems honest looking to me."

Billy Goat said, "Sometimes it's hard for me to believe you are my brother."

Smarty looked at the brothers and wondered how they became mechanics. He had learned a long time ago to never judge anything or anyone.

"My car ready?" he asked.

"Yep. Good as new."

He reached into his pocket and removed a money clip. Their eyes almost jumped out of their head. The clip was full. It would not have held another dollar.

Willie handed him a bill. He didn't hesitate. He looked at it and pulled two bills from the clip. He turned and started toward his car.

"Hey, mister," Willie said. "You forgot your change."

"Keep it as a tip for doing the job."

"Thanks!" Willie said.

Smarty started his car and drove down the street toward the Shady Nook Inn. Tomorrow was going to be a long day but one he was looking forward to.

## Fame and Fortune Awaits Elmer

With everything settled, Smarty pulled out from Smallville early the next morning. Elmer sat beside him with a frightened look on his face.

"Hey, kid, don't look so frightened," Smarty said.

"Yes, sir, but I can't help it. I have never been away from my parents and brother and sister."

"You will get used to it, kid."

"I don't know, sir."

"Come on, kid. Once you're in the big village, and you are dancing, it will become easier."

"You may be right, sir."

"Buck up, kid. Everything will work out all right."

"Sir, I wish you would not call me *kid*."

"If you don't call me *sir*, I will not call you *kid*."

"Deal," Elmer said, sticking out his hand. Smarty took his hand in a firm grip.

Neither knew it at the time, but with the handshake a bond was formed between them that would last a lifetime. Elmer sat quietly watching the country roll by. He had no idea where he was going, but he trusted Smarty, so he didn't worry.

Elmer spoke asking, "If I don't say *sir* and then when I want to talk to you, what do I call you?"

"My name is *Smarty*."

"Smarty Fox," Elmer said. "I like that. That's a good name to have."

Smarty smiled at what Elmer had said. He knew that not only was he going to be his promoter, but he was going to be his friend. In his mind he knew that no one would ever take advantage of him as long as he was around. He knew that Elmer was still young but was plenty smart for his age. He drove in silence, for Elmer had put the seat back and was asleep.

Elmer lay back in the seat and pretended to be asleep, but he was thinking of home. He had been gone only two days but was already missing them. He could see his mother and father smiling at him. His brother's and sister's faces came into his mind, and he felt a twinge in his heart. He knew that he could not go back, for he had told Smarty he would dance for him in the big village. Dance he would, the likes that had never been seen before in the big village.

The journey was long and tiring, but finally they arrived at the big village. Elmer sat up, taking in everything around him. He could not believe the size of some of the buildings. There were buildings almost the size of Smallville. He had never dreamed that such things existed.

"What you think of the big village?" Smarty asked.

"I have never imagined that there was any place this big."

"See this building on your right? The one with the long sign on it. That is the largest theater in the village. There is where you will dance."

Elmer's eyes grew large as he looked at the huge building. He was amazed as Smarty pulled in and parked the car. Smarty got out and came around to Elmer's side. He opened  the door and motioned for him to get out. Elmer hesitantly stepped out, still looking up.

"Quite a building," he said, looking at Smarty.

"One of the tallest in the Animals  Kingdom."

Smarty placed his hand on Elmer's shoulder. They began to walk toward the doors. They opened. Elmer jumped back, for he had never seen doors that automatically opened.

Smarty chuckled. "Come," he said. "They will not  hurt  you.  They  will   open  for  you automatically."

With his hand on Elmer's shoulder he steered him toward the center of a huge room. He was watching his face as they walked. *He will take some watching until he gets used to the ways of the big villages*, he thought. Then a thought entered his mind. His sister Foxie Fox could be made his guardian until he became educated to the facts of life in the big village.

Smarty led Elmer over to a door that read, "Elevator." The door opened, and Smarty stepped inside of a small room. Elmer followed.

Then to the amazement of Elmer, the room began to move upward. He stood still. He didn't want Smarty to see that he was scared. The room stopped moving, and the door opened.

He moved out into a huge room in front of Smarty. Smarty smiled and started toward a closed door. He stopped in front of the door and pointed toward the writing on it. Elmer read, "Fox, Fox & Fox promoters."

"What does that mean?" he asked.

## Foxie Fox

"It means that my brother and sister and I are the biggest promoters of show business in the world. They run the office part of the business, and I work the field, hunting the talent. That's how I found you, my boy, out in the field going village to village."

He opened the door, and Elmer followed him. There, sitting at a desk, was a lady fox. Elmer looked at her. He couldn't believe his eyes. This was one of the prettiest fox ladies he had ever seen. She came from behind the desk and hugged Smarty.

"Hey, big brother. What did you bring us this time?"

"I bring to the showplace of the nation the most sensational act the world has ever seen."

"Sure you do. You have flunked out with the last two. What makes you think you have hit the Big Time now?"

"Come around here, Elmer, where she can see you."

Elmer stepped around in front of Smarty to where he could be seen. Foxie came around and began to walk around Elmer. "Hmm," she said. "Not bad looking for a man turtle. What can he do that makes him outstanding?"

"He dances like no one you have ever seen."

"I bet," Foxie said, going back around the desk. "I will have to let John in on this."

"Good," Smarty said. "Bring the old geezer in. He needs something in his life to pep him up."

John was the oldest of the three. He ran the business part of the business. Smarty hunted for the talent part of the show. Foxie saw to the schedules and the welfare of their acts. John knew his way around all the big producers of the village. Foxie pressed a buzzer on her desk.

"What?" a gruff voice came over the intercom.

"Your favorite brother is here with new talent."

"New talent my eye. He hasn't had any type of act here lately that made it overnight."

## John Fox

"Big brother, you are in for a surprise this time," Smarty said with a chuckle.

The intercom grew quiet, and Smarty turned to Elmer and said, "Don't be surprised at the way he acts. He puts on the appearance of being tough. At heart he an old softie."

A door opened behind Elmer, and he turned as a huge fox came in to the room. He was wearing a dark suit, and his stomach hung over his belt.

Elmer thought this was the biggest man fox he had ever seen. His hair was solid white, and he wore a pair of glasses on the end of his nose.

He walked over to Elmer and looked down at him. He turned and went over toward the desk and then turned real fast, staring at Elmer.

Smarty bent down and whispered in Elmer's ear.

"Don't be intimidated by him. He uses this on all new talent."

He went around the desk and sat down in a huge chair that he filled. Taking off his glasses and cleaning them, he stared at Elmer.

"What can he do?" he asked.

"He dances in a way that you have never seen."

"Dance, huh?"

"Yes, dance, and like I said, in a way you have never seen."

"Foxie, take the young man, settle him in, and get him some food. Call down and get the stage set up since there is no scheduled show tonight."

He looked at Elmer and smiled. "Go with Foxie and rest for a while. We will call you when we are ready for you."

"Yes, sir," Elmer said as he turned and followed Foxie from the room.

John turned to Smarty, looking down his nose though his glasses.

"Is he good?"

"John, this kid is the best I have ever seen. He is the most sensational dancer you will ever see. The story is he came into this world with a smile on his face, dancing."

"Say, Smarty," John said. "That's good, real good. I see it now." He moved his hand though the air in a circle. "I can see it in the lights on the marquis.

## Elmer the Dancing Turtle

## Born with a smile on his face

## And his feet

## Dancing

Elmer the dancing turtle was then born in the minds of two of the greatest promoters that ever lived--Smarty and John Fox.

Elmer followed Foxie down the hall. She came to a room and opened the door.

"This is where you will live while with us," she said. "I will have you some food sent up. Your belongings that you brought with you are in the bedroom. By the time you get a shower, the food will be ready for you."

Elmer watched as she closed the door, leaving him there all along. He turned and started for the bathroom. He felt that the one thing he needed most in the world was a nice warm bath. A hot bath and a warm meal, and Elmer felt tired. He sat down in a large chair. He had intended to rest a while and then lie down and get a nap. In a few minutes he was in a deep sleep.

How long he had been asleep? He didn't know, but he was awakened by someone calling his name. He opened his eyes to see Smarty smiling down at him.

"Go put your outfit on. We have an audition set up for you."

"You mean I am finally going to get to dance?"

"You are and on a stage the likes you have never seen. Now scoot and get dressed."

Elmer jumped up and danced across the floor to the bedroom where his outfit had been laid out for him. His heart was pounding with excitement as he dressed. Dressed with hat and cane in his hands, he danced out into the room with Smarty. A big smile lit up Smarty's face. They started out into the hallway with a smile on Smarty's face and Elmer dancing beside him.

Elmer was shown a door that said, "Stage Entrance, Authorized Personnel Only." He followed Smarty through the door and to his amazement onto one of the largest stages he had ever seen.

"Check it out," Smarty said. "No one else is here at this time. Go over and check it out good, for when the lights are off, and the spots come on, it will be a different world."

Elmer danced from one end of the stage to the other. Then he did a few crisscrosses and came back to Smarty.

"What you think?" he asked Elmer.

"This is one of the most wonderful floors that I have ever seen."

A door in the theater opened, showing a light into the seating section of the theater.

"Quick! Come with me," Smarty said, hustling Elmer off the stage and behind the curtain.

"When that curtain goes up, show them what you can do. Nothing fancy. Do just what comes naturally."

Smarty stepped from behind the curtain and spoke to the audience.

"Ladies and gentleman, I now give to you the wonder of the century, the turtle that was born with a smile on his face and his feet dancing. Elmer the Dancing Turtle."

The music started, and the curtain began to part. Elmer watched Smarty for his cue to go on stage. Smarty raised his hand, and as the curtain came open he dropped his hand. That was Elmer's cue.

He put a red shoe around the curtain where it could be seen. The spotlight hit the shoe, and the audience went quiet. Then a hat. Next came a cane, and the audience was leaning forward trying to see who was behind the curtain.

Then Elmer came out dancing, the crowd went wild. They were yelling and clapping. Then as Elmer went into his dance, they grew quiet. Elmer gave them what they had come to see. They talked about him for years after he left the big village.

## The Good Life for Elmer

That was his first night, but days rolled into months. Months turned into years. During the off season, for the theater he was busy doing commercials for different companies. He starred in movies and was known everywhere for his charitable work.

Smarty watched him change from the happy, free young fellow to a man who had a lot on his mind. He had on several occasions tried to talk to him about it. He was brushed aside and told that he was all right. Smarty knew that he wasn't all right and feared that there might be a health problem. The one thing that Smarty noticed was that no matter what was asked of him, he was willing to help a fellow man. Those that worked with him would tell you that Elmer was an angel.

Smarty carried him to the doctor and had him given a physical. The doctor said he was a very healthy turtle but needed to slow his life down. He said the fast life was going to catch up with him.

Elmer had done his last show of the season, and he and the Fox trio went out for supper. They had finished eating and were sitting around the table talking.

"Elmer, you have any plans for the slack season coming up?" Smarty asked.

"Yes, I do."

"What is on your mind?" John asked.

Elmer said one word. "Home."

"Home," Foxie said. "No, you are going to stay here, and we will take in all the nightclubs. We will paint this old village red this season."

Elmer stood up. "Going to turn in early. Got my car packed and ready, I will leave early in the morning. Won't have time to say good-bye, so I will do it now."

He shook hands with Smarty and then John. Foxie stood up and hugged him.

"Wish you would stay. We could have more good times."

"I'm sure we could, Foxie, but I want to see my mother and father and brother and sister."

Smarty watched as he left the room. He was glad to see that he was going home. He had a feeling that something was about to happen that would change everything.

John looked over at Smarty. "You feel it also?" he asked. Smarty shook his head and looked at Foxie's tears running down her cheeks.

"He won't be back," she said, dabbing a handkerchief at her eyes. "Stop him. Don't let him go."

They watched with sad hearts as the door closed behind him.

Smarty knew that Elmer would never dance on stage in the big village again. He also knew that he would see his little friend again.

Elmer left the room with a heavy heart, for he knew that he was leaving some of the best friends that a person could ever have. You see, in his heart he knew that he would never dance on the big stage again.

## Elmer, Home at Last

*Lonie B. Adcock*

# Home is Where the Heart Is

Elmer wasted no time the next morning. His car was ready and waiting for him. He headed out of the big village and to the place in his heart-- Smallville. He listened to the radio and, as he got closer to home, began to sing. His feet were moving on the floorboard to the music. He knew that it would take another day before he got home, so he checked in a travel lodge for the night. This was the same one he and Smarty stayed in the first night when he had left home.

The next morning found him on the road with anxiety in his heart. He wondered if his people would accept him after all these years. How would the people of Smallville treat him. *How* ran through, his mind. He was so engrossed in his thoughts that he hadn't noticed that he was going around Forbidden Mountain that sat a few miles from Smallville. The kids in Smallville were told that they would never return if they wandered up on the mountain. No one in Smallville knew what was on the mountain.

He was so deep in thought that when the creature flew in front of his car that it startled him, and he hit his brakes, coming to a sudden stop. He sat still for a few moments. Then he opened the door and stepped out. He looked around. Nothing was in sight. He sat back down in the car and closed the door. He started out in the road, moving slowly, watching everything around him.

He knew that he had seen something that didn't exist. He had seen a small human with wings fly in front of his car. All the pictures he had seen of humans had no wings. The size of what he saw was no larger than he was. All humans were large and had big feet that would step on you if you didn't get out of the way. This creature looked like a human with wings, and long golden hair. Coming over a small hill, he saw Smallville in the distance. He would be there in just a few more minutes. He drove down the main street of Smallville. At that time of day there weren't but several residents of the village out. He passed the garage of Billy and Willie Goat. They looked up from a car as Elmer passed.

"Look, Willie, a big villager dude."

"I see him, Billie, but that wasn't no big villager dude."

"Was so. I saw him with my own eyes."

"I don't care what you saw with your own eyes. Weren't no big villager dude."

"If you so smart, Mr. Willie Goat, who was it then?"

"That," Willie said, removing his ball cap and scratching his head, "was Elmer."

"Who do you say that is?"

"That was Elmer the Dancing Turtle."

"You don't say," Billie said, wiping his face with a greasy rag. Realizing that he had wiped grease all over his face, he turned and started inside. "Will miracles never cease?"

Elmer pulled to a stop in front of his parents' house. It looked the same as when he left. He opened the door and stepped out on the ground. He looked around and didn't see anyone. He closed the door and started toward the house. He danced to the door as he had always done. The door flew open, and Lulu came running toward him with her arms stretched out. She embraced him in a hug that made Elmer think she was going to break his ribs.

"My boy!" she cried with the tears running down her face. Elmer held her in a tight hug.

"Hello, Mom," he said, kissing her on the forehead.

"My boy!" Lulu kept repeating. "Are you home to stay?" she asked, looking him in the face.

"Mom, only time will tell if I go back to the big village or not. I am home, and I intend to be here at least to the end of the season."

Placing her hands on his arm, she said, "Come. You must be hungry."

"Only if you got some of my favorite greens cooked."

"That's strange, for I was thinking of you this morning. I got up, and for some reason I cooked up a pot of your favorite greens."

Inside, Elmer sat at the table, eating his greens and a piece of acorn nut bread. Lulu sat across the table with a big smile on her face and watched him. He looked a lot older than she had imagined he would. It must have been the hard work that made him look that way.

"Mom, where are Pop and Hiram and Myrtle?"

"Your father is down at the school, helping Professor Hootie get the auditorium ready for Saturday night."

"What is happening Saturday night?"

"It's the graduating class getting their diploma and a show afterward."

"Good. Professor Hootie is one of the best men I have ever met. He's always ready to help out a fellow man."

"He is getting old, but his son is just like him. When the time comes, he will be able to take over. You remember Toot his daughter? She now teaches school."

"Where are Hiram and Myrtle?" he asked again.

"Why, Elmer, have you forgotten that I wrote and told you when your sister and brother got married? Hiram has a little boy, and Myrtle has a set of twins girls."

Lulu saw a strange look on Elmer's face. He looked as if he hadn't heard when they got married.

"Must have slipped my mind."

Elmer knew that he had not received any mail from his mother. He talked to her over the communication system while he was away. He was sure he had not received a letter. He bet Foxie got it and threw it away so he wouldn't come back for the weddings. She was afraid that if he came home he would not return. It didn't matter. He was home now. It was at that moment that he knew he was going to stay in Smallville. No going back to the big village, ever.

Lulu helped him unpack his suitcases, and everything was put away. It seemed strange being in such a small room after what he was used to. He told Lulu he was going to Professor Hootie's to see his dad. Lulu smiled as he pulled out, heading back to the village. She smiled, for her boy had come home.

Roscoe and Hootie were on stage and didn't see Elmer when he came in. They were on the far side of the stage from him. He eased out onto the stage, and then he began to dance. Professor Hootie and Roscoe turned around.

With a surprised look on his face, Roscoe started to run toward Elmer. They met in the middle of the stage. They stood still hugging each other. Finally Roscoe stood back looking at him.

"My boy has come home!" he said, loud enough for Professor Hootie to hear.

Elmer danced over to where the professor was standing, sticking out his hand to him. The Professor took it with a grip that surprised Elmer.

"Glad to see you back," the professor said.

"Good to be back, sir," he answered. "Be here for a while."

Elmer danced over to where Roscoe stood watching him.

"Ready to go, Pop?" he asked.

"Ready, son" he said, waving to Professor Hootie.

Roscoe walked outside in the sunlight. That was when he noticed how Elmer had aged. He didn't say anything, for he was so happy to have him there by his side. They got in the car, and Elmer headed back home.

"Have you seen your brother and sister since you got back?" Roscoe asked.

"Not yet, Pop. Mom said she would call them and let them know that I was here. If they aren't at home, we will go and find them."

Elmer drove the rest of the way in silence. It had been so long since he had seen his father that he was a stranger. He would have to get used to his family again. He loved his family, and he couldn't understand how he had stayed away so long. He pulled into the driveway, and he noticed that there were several more cars there. He could hardly wait to see his brother and sister. He had been close to them, growing up.

As he parked the car, the door came open in the front of the house. Hiram and Myrtle came running out. By the time he was out of the car, Myrtle had him hugged. She looked up with tears in her eyes.

"It's been a long time, big brother, since I last saw you."

"Too long, little sister," Elmer said, hugging her tightly.

"Hey, little brother. Don't you have a hug for your older brother?"

Elmer looked at Hiram and noticed that he had put on a big stomach. He hugged him and whispered, "Looks like that easy living has given you something to hang over your belt."

Hiram let out a booming laugh. "Worked hard to get that," he said, patting his stomach.

Elmer looked down at two little ones standing, watching their mother.

"Hey," he said, "where did these small tikes come from?"

Myrtle said, "Come over here and meet your uncle Elmer."

They walked over really slowly and looked up at Elmer. He squatted down, reached out, and hugged them.

"What are your names?" he asked.

"I am Bennie," the little one wearing the baseball cap said.

"I am Minnie," the other said, shyly.

He stood up and, turning to say something to Hiram, felt a tug on his leg. Looking down he saw a small boy looking up at him. Then to his surprise the boy did a two step backward and began to dance. A surprised look came on Elmer's face. When he looked down at the dancing boy, he saw another dancer—himself.

Hiram let out one of his booming laughs and said, "Meet your namesake."

"My namesake?" Elmer asked.

"Your namesake, for he acts the way you did when we were growing up. He never walks like everyone else. He dances everywhere he goes, so it was natural that he be named Elmer. Now I want you to meet my wife, Josie."

Elmer hugged her and smiled at Hiram in approval. Hiram's face lit up, for he was proud of his wife.

Myrtle stepped forward saying, "Elmer, this is my husband, Joe."

Elmer shook hands with Joe and realized that Joe and Josie were twins.

They all went into the house, everyone talking at the same time. Lulu had the table set, and it was full of everyone's favorite. They all sat down and waited, for they knew that no one ate until Roscoe blessed their food.

They bowed their heads, and Roscoe spoke.

"All mighty Creator of the universe, we thank you for bringing our boy back home. We are thankful for the mighty blessings you have bestowed upon us. You have given Mama and me a lovely family, and they have in turn given us lovely grand-kids. For all the things that you have given, we thank you." Roscoe paused and said, "We thank you for returning our son home. Oh mighty

Creator, we want you to bless this food, and in your name, Amen."

It was quiet at the table. No one spoke. They were all looking at Elmer who still had his head bowed. They saw a tear run down his cheek. He straightened up and looked at them. A smile lit up his face.

He spoke, saying, "Don't pay any attention to me, I am happy to be back home with my family. I should have never left in the first place. Now let's eat before Mom's food gets cold."

The next few days were spent getting to know old friends again. He tried not to miss any of his old classmates. He thought he had seen them all, but he had not seen Bucky Beaver. He was told that Bucky had an old truck and hauled lumber for his father's sawmill. He would go and sit in the park, relaxing and watching the kids play.

**Bucky Mo Bile**

He was sitting on a bench, relaxed, when he heard a loud noise. Turning, he saw an old truck stopping in the parking lot. Then the door opened, and a figure stepped out. He shook his head. There was no mistaking who it was. The ball cap, turned sideways on his head, gave him away. He came down to where Elmer sat and stopped in front of him.

"Well, well," he said with a sneer. "Elmer the wonder boy."

"Hello, Bucky," Elmer said, extending his hand to him.

He looked at the hand and spat on it.

"That's what I think of your stinking hand."

He turned and with a loud laugh started back toward his truck. He stopped and turned back to Elmer, asking, "You want to make something out of what I just done?"

Elmer shook his head, wiping off his hand.

"Someday, Bucky, the things you do to others will come back home to you."

Giving Elmer what was called a horse laugh, he jumped into the truck and left, squealing tires out of the parking lot.

Professor Hootie had asked Elmer to dance for them in the show that was being put on at the auditorium. He had agreed to and was sitting in the dressing room when Professor Hootie stuck his head into the room.

"Ready, Elmer?" he asked.

"Yes, sir," Elmer said. He turned to the professor, asking, "What is it with the weather?"

"We have a bad storm headed our way, but I think everything will be all right."

"Sure hope so," Elmer said, getting up and going out to where he could see the stage. The children were performing, and the auditorium was full. He started to turn back to Professor Hootie when the lights went out.

It sounded like an explosion, and then things began to fly through the air. The children on the stage began to scream and run. He ran onto the stage and began to gather the children around him. As he began to tell them to follow him, a timber hit the center of the stage just as he got the children off.

With the children outside where it was safe, he headed back inside for he knew that the professor was still inside. He made his way through the fallen timbers until he came to the professor. Helping the professor, he started outside with him. He placed the professor with the kids and headed back inside. It never occurred to him that he was placing his life in danger. He knew that there were others inside, and he was going to help them.

He had heard a moan in the front row as he was leaving with the professor. He made his way around the stage and to the front row of seats. Then he heard it again. He stopped trying to place where the moan had come from. Then from underneath a curtain he heard the moan again. He ran over and began to look behind the curtain where the moan had came from.

There he saw what he could never make a mistake in knowing what it was. It was Bucky Beaver's ball cap.

"Bucky!" he began to yell, as he was moving timbers and trash from him. "Bucky, can you hear me?"

"Yes," came a faint voice. "I hear you."

A rumble, and then a large timber fell from the ceiling onto the stage.

Bucky let out a loud scream.

Everyone had gotten outside safely but were told by Professor Hootie how Elmer went back inside to help someone. Everyone was accounted for, and they could not imagine who else was inside that Elmer had gone back for. A loud rumble, and they knew that the roof was falling in on who was inside.

A piece of wood hit Elmer, knocking him down, but he jumped up, wiping blood from his face. He began to pull the broken lumber from Bucky.

"Hang in there, Bucky. I am coming."

"Go, Elmer," Bucky said. "Go while you can. Go! The whole roof is falling in."

Then the hand that Bucky had spit on just a few days back reached down and took him by the shoulder.

"Where are you hurt?" he asked.

"Don't think I am hurt. My leg is pinned under a beam."

Elmer moved around to where he could see Bucky's leg.

"Easy," he said, as he begin to move broken pieces of lumber from his leg. A rumble, and the back section of the building fell. Pieces of lumber and other building material blew up into the air.

They all stood outside safely away from the building, watching it fall in. There was no doubt in their minds that Elmer and the other one in the building were dead. Elmer's mother and father stood huddled together with Hiram and Myrtle.

Elmer had removed everything from Bucky's leg but a large timber. He tried to lift it but could not.

"Get out of here!" Bucky kept telling Elmer.

Elmer grabbed a short piece of timber and placed it under the beam that had Bucky pinned down. Then with everything in his body, he pried down on it. The beam moved, and Bucky moved his foot from under it.

"I am free!" he shouted to Elmer.

Elmer slowly let the timber down. Then as he straighten up the roof began to fall in again. A piece of wood hit him, twisting him around and throwing him to the ground. Something popped in  his right leg as he fell. Bucky heard the popping noise and ran around the beam to find Elmer lying on the floor.

"Elmer!" Bucky yelled as he bent over and picked him up. Bucky looked at him and knew he was dead.

The roof was still falling and he began to run and jump over stuff lying in the floor. He could see the front door. The door was open, and he ran though it with Elmer in his arms. He got to safety, laying Elmer down gently on the ground.

The crowd rushed to help him. He collapsed beside Elmer. He wasn't hurt. He was just exhausted.

"Get him to the hospital!" he yelled to the crowd.

Elmer was removed, and then they helped Bucky to his feet. He looked around at them and then began to run toward the hospital. He ran inside looking for Elmer. They stopped him in the hallway. A nurse took him to a room and told him to wait there. She left, and in a few minutes came back with Elmer's family. They sat down not saying anything at first.

Roscoe looked at Bucky and spoke.

"I want to thank you for saving my boys life."

Bucky spoke in a voice that they could not believe  was his. "I didn't save his life. He saved mine. I tried to get him to leave me, but he wouldn't go. The building was falling down on us, but he wouldn't leave me. A piece of lumber hit him just as he freed me. I heard his leg pop as he fell to the floor. Mister Turtle, if he dies it will be my fault." Tears rolled down his cheeks.

Roscoe reached out and took hold of his shoulder. "Don't feel that way," he said. "Elmer did what he knew he had to do."

"I have done some awful things to him, Mister Turtle. It has only been a few days back that he wanted to shake hands with me. He reached out his hand to me, and I spat on it."

Bucky got up and went over to the door and stared though the glass. The door opened. He stepped back. Doctor Foggers Frog came in. He looked around, and then he saw Bucky.

"You Bucky Beaver? Elmer wanted to know if you got out okay. He was worried that you had been hurt. Elmer's going to be okay. He has a slight concussion. The big hurt is his right foot at the ankle. There is a torn ligament. This will keep him from ever dancing again. You may go in to see him but don't stay long, for he needs to rest."

They left the room, following Doctor Frog. The door was open, and Elmer lay still on a bed. They walked in and gathered around the bed. Bucky hesitated in the doorway. Lulu reached out and took his hand and led him on in the room. He looked down at Elmer, and tears rolled down his cheeks. Lulu saw them and knew he was hurting on the inside. She reached out and moved him closer to the bed.

Elmer opened his eyes and saw Bucky and asked, "You okay?"

Bucky wiped his eyes and shook his head *yes*.

"That was horrible in there, wasn't it?"

"I have never been so scared in all my life as I was when you came to me. I knew that I was going to die." Bucky shook his head. "I can't imagine why you wanted to help me after the way I treated you all these years."

"Aww! You're not such a bad guy. I have never held anything you did against you."

Old Doctor Frog came into the room and ushered them out. They left, going home with the understanding that they could see Elmer early the next morning.

Elmer left the hospital a few days later. He had to walk on crutches. The news that old Doctor Frog had given him was disturbing. He had been told by the doctor that the tendons and ligaments were stretched out of shape in his foot. He would never be able to walk normal again. The one thing that the old doctor had made clear--he would never dance again. When he told Elmer that he would never dance again, it took something out of him. Dancing was what he had lived for.

He would go out to the park every day and sit and watch the kids play. His namesake, Little Elmer, could be seen dancing all around the park. He walked around town talking to people and saw the look of pity in their eyes. They all knew that dancing was his life, and knowing he could never do it again brought pity to their faces.

They had almost finished rebuilding the auditorium. Bucky with his old truck had hauled most of the lumber from the yard that his father ran. Bucky had changed since that night. He never failed to look up Elmer during the day and sit and talk to him. He had become one of the politest and nicest creatures in Smallville. Elmer knew that he blamed himself for what happened to him. Elmer tried to tell him that it wasn't his fault. He blamed no one. What had made the auditorium crumble had been a tornado. No one could have seen it coming.

# The Forbidden Mountain

On the east side of Smallville was a large mountain. Ever since he was a kid he had been told to never go up on top of it. Stories were told of creatures that lived on the mountain that would take your life. Elmer remembered that he had seen a creature of some kind on the road as he came home. What he had seen looked like a human with wings. It was too small to be a human.

Elmer got up before his parents were awake and left the house. He had his dancing outfit that the professor had given him in a bag. He got to the professor's office and opened the door and went inside. He had hoped he wouldn't run into him. He laid the outfit down on the desk and taking out a note placed it on top of it. He left, closing the door very softly as not to disturb the professor.

He left the professor's office and headed straight for the mountain. He reached the base of the mountain, exhausted. He sat down on a fallen tree to rest. He leaned back against a limb on a tree. He closed his eyes and was almost asleep when a fluttering noise made him sit up. He looked around but didn't see anything. He looked around to see if a bird was close by. Nothing moved or made any noise. *Must have been asleep,* he thought.

Elmer set out again, going up the mountain at a snail's pace. It was rough going, especially on crutches. It began to get dark, so he looked around for a place to spend the night. Finding a hollow log, he crawled in and lay down. He was tired from the mountain climbing and fell asleep in a few seconds.

He awoke and realized it was daylight. He crawled from the log and began the trek up the hill. He picked berries and ate them to do away with his hunger. Then he heard it again--the fluttering noise. He looked around. Nothing could be seen. It must be a hummingbird, for they made a fluttering noise when they flew. Then he heard what sounded like a giggle, the kind coming from a small child. He stopped and sat down, scanning the woods around him. Nothing was there except the trees and bushes of the forest. He started to walk again when he heard a rumble of thunder.

It was getting dark overhead, and the thunder and lightning were getting closer to him. He saw a ledge under a rock and made his way toward it. He could hear the rushing of water. There in front of him was a raging river. The rain from above had turned it into a swirling mass of water. All kinds of trees and trash were rushing down the river. Just as a pop of thunder and lightning struck, he made it to safety under the ledge.

Then he heard it again--a small voice. This time it was calling for help. He removed his shirt and shoes, searching the water for the voice. There in the water on a tree limb he saw it. It was a small human form hanging onto the tree which was starting to float down the river. Without giving a thought to his safety, he jumped into the water. In the water the lame foot didn't bother him without the weight on it. He reached out, grabbing the small figure from the tree just as it tore loose and went swirling down the river.

He managed somehow to get the small figure onto the rock and to safety. He laid it down on a patch of soft moss. He moved back with water dripping from him and looked at what he had dragged from the river. It was not bigger than he. It looked like a human but had a set of wings on its back. This was what he had seen that day in his car. Then he remembered the professor telling them about what was thought to live on the mountain. He called them evil fairies.

Then it began to shiver as if it were cold. He picked up his shirt and covered it up. He sat down with his back against the rock where he could watch it. He had noticed that it had long yellow hair. *Must be a female,* he said to himself.

He was exhausted, and his foot was hurting him. In a comfortable position the foot eased down, and he went to sleep. He woke up with something poking him in the stomach. He opened his eyes and couldn't believe what he saw. There all around him was a group of the creatures, looking at him with swords in their hands. He moved against the rock as the one out front punched him again. Then he drew back the long sword and started to strike Elmer.

A high pitched scream broke the silence. He held the sword in the strike position but turned to see where the scream came from. Then with a fluttering of wings, the small yellow haired  fairy  came between Elmer and the one holding the sword.

"No!" she screamed in a high pitched voice. "You will not harm him."

"No one will do any harm to this creature. He jumped in the river last night and saved my life. Anyone does him harm will answer to my father King Harrell. You know how the king feels about me, his daughter."

Then to their amazement she turned and reached out a hand to Elmer. He took it and got to his feet. She then went over to where his crutches were and brought them to him. He took them and placed them under his arms.

"Thank you for saving my life."

"Only fair. You saved mine last night. Now come. We will take you to our town."

She moved out in front of him. He began to follow her, moving slowly on the crutches. The thought that was in his mind was what was going to happen now? The state of mind that he had gotten in made him not care what happened. He no longer had any desire to go on living. The one thing that he had lived for was gone--his dancing. He was full of self pity.

## Princess Sunshine

Princess Sunshine moved slowly along in front of him. There was a feeling of caring for this creature in her heart. She had slipped from the mountain many nights and had seen him dance. Her father would be furious if he ever found out that she had disobeyed his orders. He was strict about no one leaving the mountain where the fairies lived. She had sat on the ledge of a window in the auditorium and watched him on stage dancing. Now to see him trying to get along on crutches gave her a sad feeling on the inside of her. Every so often she would turn and fly backward giving him a big smile.

Elmer watched as they approached a village the likes he had never seen. It was cut in the side of the mountain. A huge door opened, and they entered. There on the inside of the mountain were buildings of all shapes. Some huge and some really small. As he would find out later, the small one was where they lived. The other one was the *town* as they called it.

A huge building sat alone. It looked like what the humans called a castle. As he found out, it was indeed a castle. It was the castle of King Harrell, the king of the fairies, the father of Princess Sunshine.

They entered the castle and into a long hall. The floor was slick. Elmer had a hard time moving on the crutches. Odom, the Commander of the Fairies Army, poked him.

Princess Sunshine flew between them, yelling at him.

"Don't you dare ever touch him again with your sword. If you do I will tell my father. If you had to walk on those things under your arms, could you do it?"

Odom backed away from Elmer, and Princess Sunshine smiled, saying, "Come. It won't happen again."

They came through another door and into a room the likes that Elmer could only believe existed in a dream. There on a throne sat a huge fairy. He was larger in statue than the others. A crown of gold and precious

**125**

stones sat on his head. He stared down at Elmer. Elmer shrunk backward only to meet two hands in his back, keeping him where he was.

Odom stepped forward. "Sir, we found Princess Sunshine only to find this creature nearby."

King Harrell stared down at him.

Elmer stood up straight and stared back at him. He wasn't going to show any fear to him. Elmer was at the point in life that he did not care what happened to him. He wasn't going to shrink away like a coward.

King Harrell liked courage in any creature, and to see this little creature stand up straight and proud made him feel good. He hated to pronounce sentence on him, but the code of the fairies was that no one could enter their land and leave.

"Take him to the holding chamber. Keep him there until we figure out what to do with him. He is in no shape to work in the mine with a lame leg."

"No!" Princess Sunshine said, moving down in front of Elmer. "He saved my life, and for that I am grateful. I will defend him in a Council of Elders."

" You know what you are saying girl?"

"Yes, I do."

"You are willing to stand in front of the Elders and argue for the life of a creature from the outside world?"

"Yes, I am."

"Very well, girl, but I think you are being stupid to go in front of the Elders. Commander Odom, take him to a holding room until the Elders" can be contacted. Commander he is to be treated as you would want to be treated if you were him."

"Very well," Commander Odom said, turning to Elmer. "You will come with me."

Elmer heard a flutter of wings, and Princess Sunshine stood in front of him.

She gave him a big smile, saying, "Don't worry. I won't let anyone do you harm."

Elmer followed Commander Odom from the room and to the holding room. He entered the room and heard a lock click behind him. He went over to a bed and lay down. He was very tired.

## The Trial by the Elders

Elmer was awakened by Commander Odom. He was told his trial by the Elders was about to begin. He got up and, picking up his crutches, began to follow him. Commander Odom seemed to have a sneer on his face when he looked at Elmer. Elmer ignored him as he walked down the long hallway to the room of the Elders. The door opened, and Elmer walked into the room. A circle table with five old fairies sat in the middle of the room. Elmer stopped in front of them. They were very old. They looked like they were sour on the whole world.

"Who are you?" one of them asked.

"I, sir, am Elmer Turtle."

"Why have you come to our land?"

"I have been told all my life if you go to the mountain you will never return."

"You come to our land because you would never be able to return to your land?"

"Yes, sir."

"What is so bad in your land that you would leave those that love you?"

"Look at me, sir," Elmer said. "I have nothing to live for. The thing that counted most in my life is gone. I can no longer dance. I am a cripple that only sees pity in the eyes of his friends. I thought I would climb the mountain and let what happens to those who come here happen to me."

One of the Elders stood up and leaned over the table. He spoke.

"You are a pitiful excuse of a male creature. Whatever happens to you will be a just reward. You come to our land because you would never return to yours. You are a self centered creature who thinks of no one but himself. You never think of those who love you. They are the ones that you are now hurting, while you are wrapped up in self pity. What about your mother, father, sister, and brother. Think of those who love you, worrying about what happened to you. You stand in front of me, telling me about what happened to you. You think only of yourself."

He sat down, his face red after giving Elmer a piece of his mind. Elmer dropped his head, ashamed of himself. The Elder was right, for he now knew how his family must feel. He realized that what he saw in the eyes of his family and friends was not pity but hurt. They all had loved him since he was born.

He raised his head and looked at the Elders. They were all stone faced not showing emotion.

"Sir--", he said.

Without an expression on his face one of them said, "Yes?"

"Sir, what you say is true," and a tear ran down his cheek. "What you say is true. I cannot imagine what my family and friends are feeling."

One of the Elders stood up, his wings flapping like mad.

"Get him out of here!" he yelled. "Get him out of my sight! I can't stand to look at him anymore!"

Elmer dropped his head and followed Commander Odom from the room. He carried Elmer to a different room and left him. There was food on a table, so Elmer sat down and began to eat.

As Elmer left the room, the Elders looked at each other. One of them spoke

"Don't you think you came down awfully hard on the little fellow?"

"Yes, I did, but if I got the message across to him, it will be worth it."

"What are we going to do with him?"

"Just wait and see what time does for him."

They got up and started to leave the room when they heard a voice. Turning, they saw Princess Sunshine coming into the room.

"Did you have to treat him so mean?" she asked.

"Yes, Princess, I did. You see, he was swallowed by self pity. I hope that what I did makes him see it."

"What do you intend to do with him?" she asked.

"Don't know at this time, but Commander Odom don't like him. If he gets the word, he will dispose of him gladly."

"No!" she cried out. "You can't do that. He has not harmed anyone. He saved my life when I fell into the river."

Tears began to run down her face. Her heart was broken to think that they would dispose of him, he who had gotten hurt helping others, and he had jumped in the river and saved her.

"Run along, Princess," one of the Elders said. "We will decide what is best for him."

She ran from the room with her wings making a fluttering noise. She was on her way to plead for Elmer's life to her father, the king.

Elmer sat, staring out the window at the building around him. He realized that he was underground. The town, as the fairies called it, was built underground, away from the eyes of the world. He went back in to the bed and lay down. He knew he had been selfish in thinking of himself and not the ones who loved him. He could only imagine how his mother and father felt about now.

Professor Hootie waited until he was sure that Elmer was gone for good before calling his family in to read the note that he had left. They all sat silent with tears in their eyes as the professor read it to them. Professor Hootie looked at them and felt compassion for the family. He was sure that Elmer had not meant to hurt them.

He spoke, saying, "You know that no one ever returned from the mountain. We can hope and pray to the Master of the universe that he will send Elmer back to us. We will set a date when everyone in Smallville can come to the auditorium."

Elmer was escorted to a huge building that Commander Odom called the Worship Chapel. He went inside where he was met by Princess Sunshine. He sat down beside her and waited to see what was going to happen.

"Do you ever pray?" she asked.

Elmer looked at her kind of funny and asked, "What?"

"You know--pray to God, our maker."

"I have prayed to the Master of the universe."

"He is the one we call God, the Master of the universe."

When the service was over, Commander Odom led him out and to a building he said was a medical center.

Elmer had never heard of a medical center. Old Doctor Frog was the only medical person in Smallville.

He was told to sit down in an oval chair and take his shoe off. He was instructed to stick his foot in a tube like thing. The fairy doctor was almost comic to Elmer, flying around.

He left the room, telling Elmer to put his shoe back on and wait in the hall. He was soon called back in the room where the doctor was. He looked at Elmer and shook his head.

"Were you ever told what was the matter with your foot?" he asked.

"No, sir," Elmer answered.

"Was your foot ever treated?"

"No, sir."

"Someone didn't know what to do, so I am going to fix that foot to where you can walk again."

"Can you do that, sir, fix it to where I can walk without these crutches?"

"I can, and I will if you do what I say."

"Anything you say, sir, I will do it."

He flew over to a tall cabinet and took a jar of cream from it. He handed it to Elmer.

"We have a hot spring here. You will go three times a day to it. Rub some cream on your foot and placed it in the water. You will sit with your foot in the spring for an hour at a time. Think you can do that?"

"Yes, sir," Elmer answered with a smile on his face.

Elmer was led to where the spring was. The water looked like it was boiling. He wondered if it was too hot to put your foot in. He sat down and, taking off his shoe, rubbed his foot with the salve. He said to himself *here goes* as he lowered his foot into the water. It was not too hot. It was just right. He leaned back and let his foot hang down in the water. He felt a soothing, warm feeling go up his foot and into his leg.

Elmer would go to ,the prayer chapel with Princess Sunshine, and the rest of the day was spent at the hot spring. He lost count of time. His leg began to get to where he could stand on it. Then it got to where he could walk again without the crutches.

He had been to the prayer chapel, and Princess Sunshine came back with him. They sat and talked while he had his foot in the spring. He stood up, removing his foot from the water when an urge to dance hit him. Dance he did, first slowly, and then the old Elmer way. When he finished, he heard clapping. Turning to see who it was he was surprised. King Harrell, Queen Vanna, and Princess Sunshine had been watching.

King Harrell spoke. "Young man, are you ready to go back home?"

"Yes, sir," Elmer answered.

"You can go under one condition--that you will never tell anyone about us."

"You have my word, sir."

**Queen Vanna**

"There will be one more thing you will have to do."

"Whatever you say, I will do it. I can never thank you and your fairies for what you have done for me."

"You must perform a dance for my guests tonight at a party we are having."

"It will be my pleasure, sir."

That night was talked about for a long time by the guests of King Harrell. They had never seen anything like the dancing turtle. Little did Elmer realize it was the best performance he had ever done.

The next morning, Elmer was saying his thanks to everyone before he left.

Commander Odom came up to him. "Had you worried there for a while, didn't I?"

"Yes," Elmer said, extending his hand to him.

He took it and said, "Just doing my job. No hard feelings."

"None." Elmer smiled.

Elmer started down the mountain toward Smallville when he heard a fluttering of wings. He turned his head to look back, and Princess Sunshine kissed him on the forehead.

"I will miss you, little man," she said.

"I will miss you also, pretty little Sunshine."

"When you dance in the auditorium, look         up at the window."

The going was much easier going down than it was coming up on crutches. It was getting dark as he entered Smallville. He could see a gathering at the auditorium. He knew that his family would be there, so he hurried. By the time he got there, they were all inside, and the door was closed. He opened the door very slowly as not to disturb anyone. He sat down in the back where no one could see him. Professor Hootie came out on the stage.

We are here tonight to ask our Creator to bring back our beloved Elmer Turtle."

They bowed their heads, and the professor led them in prayer. Elmer got up and eased into the foyer to where the professor's office was. He went inside and to the closet. Taking out his dancing outfit, he put it on. He went the back way to the rear of the stage. They were still praying, and no one saw him come out onto the stage.

He did the toe tapping that always announced that he was there.

Professor Hootie stopped praying and turned and looked straight at Elmer. Elmer then made his grand entrance.

That night was made a holiday in Smallville. It was called Elmer Day. It is still celebrated there today. Elmer was back home this time to stay. He never had any desire to go back to the big time in the big villages. He never told anyone about the fairies on the mountain. Whenever he performed on the stage of Smallville Auditorium, he always took off his hat at the end of a dance and waved it at a window. No one knew why, but he knew that Princess Sunshine came and sat in that window.

Elmer built him a school of dancing and taught all the little ones how to dance. If you ever go through Smallville, stop off at the Elmer the Dancing Turtle--School of Dancing.

*Lonie B. Adcock*